Louis Weber, C.E.O.
Publications International, Ltd.
7373 North Cicero Avenue
Lincolnwood, Illinois 60646

Manufactured in the U.S.A.

8 7 6 5 4 3 2 1

ISBN 1-56173-885-9

A TROLL TALE

Lucky Rainbow

Written by Jane Jerrard
Illustrated by Joe Veno

PUBLICATIONS INTERNATIONAL, LTD.

Once upon a time, a baby girl troll was born. Her mother's name was Bluebell and her father's name was Dandelion. Bluebell and Dandelion thought their baby was the prettiest troll baby they'd ever seen—even though her hair was very strange.

A troll's hair should only be one color at a time, but their baby had *seven* colors of hair. They named their little girl Rainbow because of her special hair.

As Rainbow grew up, her hair became more and more colorful. Her parents always kept Rainbow's hair covered. Even though they thought Rainbow's hair was beautiful, they knew the other troll children would make fun of her because she was different.

When the day arrived for Rainbow to start school, her mother tucked her lovely, colorful hair under a big bonnet. Rainbow kissed her mother and father good-bye, and went skipping off to school, happily swinging her lunch pail.

On the first day of school, the teacher told Rainbow's class the story of the lost Crystal Cave. "Long ago, trolls were lucky," explained Miss Moss. "They got their luck from a magical cave that was made of pure crystal. But one sad day, the entrance to the cave was sealed by a rock slide. Since that day, trolls have been no luckier than anyone else."

"Aw, that's just a silly story that somebody made up," said Cloverleaf.

Rainbow didn't care if it was a made-up story. She thought the Crystal Cave sounded exciting!

On the playground after lunch, the troll children gathered around Rainbow. They wanted to know why she wore a bonnet.

"Why are you wearing a hat?" asked Acorn.

"Are you cold?" asked Peanut.

"She's probably bald!" teased Jackrabbit, as he snatched the bonnet off Rainbow's head.

The troll children were astonished. They pointed at Rainbow's colorful hair and sang, "Rainbow is a stripe-head! Rainbow is a stripe-head!"

Rainbow's face felt hot and tears filled her eyes. She ran from the noisy playground and the taunts of her classmates. She ran until she reached the cool, quiet Troll Timber Woods. She would have kept running forever, if she hadn't tripped over a small wooden box.

Rainbow brushed her tears from her face and opened the box. Inside was a map that was yellowed and crumbling with age. It was a map of Troll Timber Woods, and the Crystal Cave was right in the middle. Much to Rainbow's surprise, there were two cave entrances marked on the map!

Rainbow carefully followed the map's directions through the forest. Up ahead, just where the map said it would be, was a big stone door. As Rainbow reached out to touch it, the door swung open as if by magic!

Rainbow stepped inside. Crystals were everywhere! And the sunlight that poured through the open door made rainbows dance and shimmer all around. She had never seen anything so beautiful.

Rainbow had found the lost Crystal Cave!

Rainbow ran back to school to tell everyone about her discovery. In no time, the whole class was standing in the Crystal Cave.

"This place looks just like Rainbow's hair!" exclaimed Jackrabbit.

"You sure are lucky, Rainbow," said Walnut.

"We are all lucky," smiled Miss Moss. "Now that the Crystal Cave has been found, all trolls will be lucky once more."

One day, not long after Rainbow found the Crystal Cave, her teacher asked for quiet in the classroom. "We have a special visitor today," she said. It was the village mayor.

"Rainbow, you are a lucky little troll," said the mayor. "Because you found our cave and restored our troll luck, I hereby proclaim that the Crystal Cave will now be called Rainbow Cave!"

Rainbow smiled. She felt like the luckiest troll in the world!